P9-CCO-717

Magic
Puppy

Magic Puppy

Muddy Paws

SUE BENTLEY

Illustrated by Angela Swan

GROSSET & DUNLAP
Published by the Penguin Group
Penguin Group (USA) Inc., 375 Hudson Street, New York, New York 10014, USA
Penguin Group (Canada), 90 Eglinton Avenue East, Suite 700,
Toronto, Ontario M4P 2Y3, Canada
(a division of Pearson Penguin Canada Inc.)
Penguin Books Ltd., 80 Strand, London WC2R 0RL, England
Penguin Group Ireland, 25 St. Stephen's Green, Dublin 2, Ireland
(a division of Penguin Books Ltd.)
Penguin Group (Australia), 250 Camberwell Road, Camberwell, Victoria 3124, Australia
(a division of Pearson Australia Group Pty. Ltd.)
Penguin Books India Pvt. Ltd., 11 Community Centre, Panchsheel Park,
New Delhi—110 017, India
Penguin Group (NZ), 67 Apollo Drive, Rosedale, North Shore 0632, New Zealand
(a division of Pearson New Zealand Ltd.)
Penguin Books (South Africa) (Pty.) Ltd., 24 Sturdee Avenue,
Rosebank, Johannesburg 2196, South Africa

Penguin Books Ltd., Registered Offices:
80 Strand, London WC2R 0RL, England

If you purchased this book without a cover, you should be aware that this book is stolen property.
It was reported as "unsold and destroyed" to the publisher, and neither the author nor the
publisher has received any payment for this "stripped book."

The scanning, uploading, and distribution of this book via the Internet or via any other means
without the permission of the publisher is illegal and punishable by law. Please purchase only
authorized electronic editions and do not participate in or encourage electronic piracy of
copyrighted materials. Your support of the author's rights is appreciated.

Text copyright © 2008 Sue Bentley. Illustrations copyright © 2008 Angela Swan. Cover
illustration copyright © 2008 Andrew Farley. First printed in Great Britain in 2008 by Penguin
Books Ltd. First published in the United States in 2009 by Grosset & Dunlap, a division of
Penguin Young Readers Group, 345 Hudson Street, New York, New York 10014. GROSSET &
DUNLAP is a trademark of Penguin Group (USA) Inc. Printed in the U.S.A.

Library of Congress Cataloging-in-Publication Data is available.

ISBN 978-0-448-45045-2   20 19 18 17 16 15

To Petra—gentle sheepdog friend
and a loyal companion.

Prologue

Storm paused to drink the clear water that flowed swiftly between two banks of ice. It felt good to be back in his home world.

But the young silver-gray wolf's happiness lasted for only a moment as he thought of his mother, Canista, wounded and in hiding.

Suddenly a terrifying howl echoed in the icy wind.

"Shadow!" Storm gasped, realizing that the fierce lone wolf was close.

Storm used his magic to transform

himself quickly so he would be hidden from Shadow. There was a bright flash and a dazzling shower of golden sparks. Where Storm had been standing there now crouched a tiny fluffy black-and-white Border collie puppy with midnight-blue eyes.

Storm trembled, hoping that his puppy disguise would protect him from the evil Shadow. Keeping his little belly low to the ground, Storm crept into a clump of snow-covered bushes.

A dark shape pushed through the bushes, loosening a cloud of snow, and Storm's tiny heart missed a beat. Shadow had found him!

But instead of the lone wolf's dark-gray muzzle and pitiless black eyes,

Storm saw a familiar silver-gray face with bright golden eyes.

"Mother!" he yapped with relief.

"I am glad you are safe and well, my son, but you have returned at a dangerous time," Canista said in a warm velvety growl. She nuzzled the disguised cub's black-and-white face, but then gave a sharp wince of pain.

"Shadow's poisonous bite sapped your strength!" Storm blew out a gentle stream of tiny gold sparks, which sank into Canista's injured leg and disappeared.

"Thank you, Storm. The pain is easing. But there's no time right now for you to help me recover all my powers. You must go—Shadow is very close," Canista rumbled softly.

Sadness rippled through Storm's tiny puppy body as he thought of his dead father and litter brothers and the once proud Moon-claw wolf pack, now broken up. His midnight-blue eyes flashed with anger. "One day I will stand beside you and face Shadow!"

Canista nodded proudly. "But until then, you must hide in the other world. Use this puppy disguise and return when your magic is stronger."

Another fierce howl split the air. "I know you are close, Storm! Come out and let us finish this!" Shadow cried in an icy growl.

"Go now, Storm! Save yourself!" Canista urged.

Bright gold sparks ignited in the tiny black-and-white puppy's fur. Storm whined softly as he felt the power building inside him. Bright golden light surrounded him. And grew brighter . . .

Chapter
ONE

Beth Hollis woke up with a start and lay looking up at the unfamiliar white ceiling with its low black beams. Rain pattered against the window and she could hear animal noises and voices outside.

Gradually Beth recognized the attic bedroom in the Tail End Farm owned by her aunt and uncle. She was staying here while her parents were away.

The room was still dark and a gust of wind sent more rain drumming against the window. Beth pulled the blanket

over her head and snuggled back under
the downy warmth.

Suddenly the bedroom door swung
open. Beth heard muffled footsteps
approaching the bed and then she felt a
rush of cool air as the blanket was
pulled aside.

"Rise and shine!" cried a voice. "Mornings start early on a farm!"

"Hey!" Beth complained, sitting straight up.

Martin Badby, her tall dark-haired cousin, stood grinning mischievously down at her.

"Give that back!" Beth demanded, lunging at him with outstretched arms.

"No way!" Martin yelled, backing away. He tossed the blanket across the room out of her reach.

Beth scowled. Martin was twelve years old, older than her by three years, but he sometimes acted as if he were six. He loved playing silly jokes on people, especially his younger cousin.

"That was a really mean thing to do!" she yelled.

"Yeah? So sue me!" Martin said cheerfully. "Are you coming downstairs, or what?"

Beth sat in the middle of her bed and crossed her arms. "No, I am not! Auntie Em said I didn't have to get up early on my first day here!"

"That's only 'cause you were sulking last night. I heard you talking to your mom and dad before they left. 'Poor me. It's *so* awful that I have to stay at boring Tail End,'" he mimicked in a silly whiny little voice.

"I don't talk like that!" Beth said, feeling her cheeks turn red. "Anyway, how would you like it if you got dumped on relatives while your parents flew to England for two weeks?"

Martin rolled his eyes. "They're not going anywhere fun, are they? It's just a boring business trip."

"I still wanted to go with them," Beth murmured. She'd never been away from her parents, except for the occasional sleepover at a friend's house, and she was really going to miss them.

"Talk about selfish. I guess you didn't even think about me?" Martin grumbled.

Beth frowned, puzzled. "What about you?"

"Well, *I* have to put up with *you*, don't I? Mom and Dad have practically ordered me to look after you. Just what I wanted, my stupid spoiled cousin following me around—not!"

"Thanks a lot! I'll try not to get in your way!" Beth cried indignantly. She flung herself off the bed and stomped over to the closet. "Can you leave now, please? I want to get dressed."

"I thought you weren't getting up?" Martin teased.

"I changed my mind. Spoiled cousins do that a lot, you know!" Beth said spiritedly.

"Whatever!" Martin went out and closed the bedroom door behind him.

Beth made a face at the closed door. She'd forgotten how annoying her cousin could be and now it seemed that he wasn't happy having her here

at all. Her spirits sank even further as she thought of the two weeks stretching endlessly ahead of her.

"Morning, Beth. You're up early. Did you sleep well?" Emily Badby called from the yard as Beth stood in the open doorway of the back porch.

"Fine, thanks," Beth replied. *No thanks to Martin*, she thought.

Her aunt held a bucket of vegetables. "Goats love fresh food. It gets them in a good mood for milking. Do you want to come and watch?"

"Okay," Beth said, shrugging. She wasn't that interested in goats, but there was still so much time before breakfast and nothing else to do.

She borrowed a pair of boots and followed her aunt into the barn. A sweet musty smell of goats, dung, and warm hay greeted her. "Phew!" Beth said as she wrinkled her nose.

Emily Badby laughed. "It's a healthy farm smell. You'll get used to it."

Beth wasn't sure she wanted to. She went to look at the brown-and-white goats in their pens, down one side of the barn. "They all look a little annoyed. What kind are they?" she asked.

"Anglo-Nubians. It's their long noses and floppy ears that give them that expression," Emily explained, selecting a goat and leading it to a small wooden platform. The goat leaped up nimbly and soon Beth was watching the creamy milk foaming into a clean bucket. "I sell milk, yogurt, and cheese in the local stores," Emily said. "My dairy's next door. You can have a look around sometime, but ask me first. I have strict rules about hygiene."

Beth nodded.

When her aunt finished milking, she poured the milk through a filter into a metal churn. "I'll just take this to the dairy and then get started on breakfast."

A loud braying noise came from the back of the barn. "Oh! What's that?" Beth looked around in surprise.

Her aunt laughed. "That's Darcy, my new billy goat. He's only been here for a week or so, but he's always complaining because he isn't getting any attention."

"Can I go and say hello to him?" Beth asked.

"Yes, of course, but be—" The rest of her aunt's reply was drowned out by a loud irritable voice in the doorway.

"There you are!" Martin cried, standing aside as his mom left. "What are you hiding in here for?"

"I wasn't hiding! Auntie Em said I could watch her milking," Beth said.

Martin flicked back a strand of wet dark hair. "Anyway, Dad said I had to ask you if you wanted to come with me to take Ella for a walk." Ella was the family's old black-and-white Welsh Border collie.

"No thanks," Beth said, feeling annoyed that he'd only asked her because his dad had made him. Turning on her heel, she went toward the back of the barn. "I'm going to look at Darcy."

"Hang on! I'll come with you. Ella won't mind waiting for her walk. I have to drag her out half the time anyway. Since Dad retired her from farm work, she's really stiffened up," Martin said.

Darcy's pen was behind some straw bales. He was a handsome dark-brown goat with a white neck. "It looks like he's wearing a cute white collar!" Beth

exclaimed as Darcy lifted his head and gave an inquisitive snicker.

Martin undid the latch and gestured for Beth to go into the pen ahead of him.

Beth hesitated. "Are you sure it's safe to go in?"

"'Course," Martin said. "Are you chicken or what?"

Beth took two steps into the pen. Suddenly, she felt Martin shove her in the back and heard the gate slam shut. She shot forward and almost went sprawling in the straw.

"You idiot!" she cried, turning around just in time to see Martin jogging away through the barn. "That's not funny!" she shouted after him.

There was a noise from behind her. Beth turned to see Darcy curling his lips and eyeing her suspiciously.

She swallowed. "N-nice goat."

Darcy lowered his head. He looked like he was going to charge!

Chapter
TWO

Beth's heart rose into her mouth.
Suddenly there was a dazzling flash of
gold light and a big shower of bright
gold sparks sprinkled all around her and
Darcy. Blinded for a moment, she
rubbed her eyes. Beth tensed as she felt
a peculiar warm, tingly feeling down
her spine.

When she could see again, she
noticed that Darcy was frozen where he
stood and standing between the goat's
legs was a tiny fluffy black-and-white
puppy with enormous midnight-blue

eyes. Specks of gold dust seemed to be glimmering around its fur.

"What's going on?" Beth exclaimed.

The tiny puppy drew itself up. "I am Storm, of the Moon-claw pack. I have arrived from a place that is far from here."

"Y-you can talk?" Beth gasped in total amazement.

Suddenly, Beth had a realization. This

was obviously another one of her cousin's practical jokes. She looked around, expecting Martin to jump out triumphantly.

But there was no sign of him. Beth slowly looked back to where Storm was blinking up at her, and Darcy was still standing as if he were carved from stone.

"I don't get this," she said, puzzled.

The fluffy black-and-white puppy took a few steps toward her on big soft paws that seemed too large for his tiny body. "I used my magic to stop this animal before it could hurt you," Storm woofed. "Who are you?"

"I'm B–Beth H–Hollis," Beth stammered.

Storm bowed his head. "I am honored to meet you, Beth."

Beth was still having trouble taking all of this in. "Um . . . me too. But . . . who are you? *What* are you?"

Storm didn't answer. Instead, there was another bright golden flash.

"Oh!" Beth found herself outside Darcy's pen. Behind her the goat snickered contentedly and she heard him moving around in the straw as if nothing had happened.

Beth looked around for the puppy. But it had disappeared and standing in its place outside the pen with her there crouched a magnificent young silver-gray wolf with glowing midnight-blue eyes. Large gold sparks glowed in the

23

thick ruff around his neck.

Beth gasped, eyeing the wolf's sharp teeth. "Storm?"

"Yes, it is me, Beth. Do not be afraid," Storm said in a deep velvety growl.

Before Beth could get used to the sight of the amazing young wolf there was a final dazzling flash of gold light

and Storm was once again a tiny fluffy black-and-white puppy.

"Wow! That's an amazing disguise. No one would ever know you're a wolf!" Beth exclaimed. "But who are you hiding from?"

Storm began to tremble all over and his deep-blue eyes glowed with anger and fear. "Shadow is a fierce lone wolf who killed my father and all my brothers and wounded my mother with his poisonous bite. Now Shadow is looking for me. Can you help me, Beth?"

"Of course I will!" Beth's soft heart went out to him. Storm was impressive as a young wolf, but he was adorable as a tiny helpless puppy. She bent down to

25

pick him up. "I'll ask Auntie Em if you can stay in my room," she said, petting his soft little ears.

Storm leaned up to lick her chin. "Thank you, Beth."

"Just wait until I tell Martin about you! He's going to be so jealous!"

"No, Beth! You can't tell anyone my secret!" Storm said, his tiny black-and-white face was very serious.

Beth didn't want to do anything that would put her new friend in danger. Besides, she reasoned, Martin had been such a pain recently that he didn't deserve to know about Storm anyway. "Okay, then," she decided. "It's just you and me. I promise."

"Aren't you a little too old to be

talking to an imaginary friend?" Martin
said, suddenly appearing from behind
the straw bales. His eyes widened when
he saw Storm. "Where did that cute
puppy come from?"

"I just found him. He said his
name's—" Beth stopped quickly as she
realized that she was going to have to
be a lot more careful about keeping
Storm's secret. "I mean I'm going to
call him Storm."

Martin's face softened for an instant. "Ella looked just like that when she was a puppy. He must be a Border collie, too. Let me hold him."

"I think I'll hold on to him. He's still a little scared," Beth said.

Martin frowned. "No one would think he's yours. This is my barn, so Storm obviously belongs to me. Hand him over!" he ordered.

Beth hesitated, annoyed at being bossed around again. Martin didn't even bother to ask if she was okay after he'd shoved her into Darcy's pen.

"Do not worry, Beth. Do as he says," Storm woofed.

Beth blinked in astonishment. What was Storm doing, talking to her when

Martin was so close? But her cousin
didn't seem to have noticed anything
strange. *I hope you know what you're
doing, Storm*, she thought as she
reluctantly held him out toward Martin.

Smiling triumphantly, Martin went to
grab Storm, but the moment he
touched his black-and-white fur he
jumped backward. "Ye-oww!" he yelled,
shaking his hands in the air. "Something

just stung me! Does he have a stinging bug in his fur or something?"

Beth pulled Storm back and held him closely again. "I'll take a look. Maybe you should go and ask Auntie Em for some antiseptic cream."

"Er . . . yeah," Martin nodded as he went off, still rubbing at his hands.

"Storm!" Beth scolded gently. "You gave him a prick from your invisible gold sparks, didn't you?"

Storm's blue eyes twinkled mischievously. "I think I may have made them a bit too sharp. But the feeling will soon wear off," he woofed.

"Serves Martin right. Maybe he'll think twice before grabbing you again! But how come he didn't hear you speak to me just now?" Beth asked, puzzled.

"I used my magic, so that only you can hear me." Storm snuggled up in Beth's arms.

"You can do that? So I can hear you, but everyone else just hears you barking? Cool!" Beth kissed the top of his soft little head. "Let's go and find Auntie Em. Breakfast should be almost ready. I bet you're hungry after your long journey."

Storm's tummy rumbled and he gave an eager little bark.

As Beth went toward the farmhouse, she smiled. Her boring two weeks at Tail End Farm looked like they were going to be a lot more fun with Storm around!

Chapter
THREE

"I wonder where he came from," Emily said thoughtfully after Beth finished telling her about Storm. "We're pretty far from any houses out here."

Beth looked across to where Storm was chomping on a dish of dog food. Ella, the old collie, lay curled in her basket watching the puppy.

"I bet Storm was abandoned. His owners were probably hoping some kind person would give him a home. Like you, Auntie Em," Beth said hopefully.

"I really hate people who treat animals like that," Martin said.

"Me too!" Beth said with feeling. It was the first time she and Martin had agreed on anything.

They all sat at the kitchen table, eating their huge farmhouse breakfasts and drinking big mugs of tea.

"I'm not sure it's a good time to have a stray puppy getting under everyone's feet," Beth's uncle said. "We're very busy on the farm and no one has time to train him. Maybe we should take Storm straight to the pet care center."

Beth's heart pounded. He couldn't mean it! She just found Storm—she couldn't bear to lose her new friend so quickly.

Suddenly Ella gave a rusty-sounding
bark. She got up and limped stiffly over
to Storm. The tiny puppy whined softly,
wagging his tail and wriggling his fat
little body as the old dog bent down
and gave him an experimental sniff.
Ella's eyes softened and she began
licking Storm's head.

Martin's face lit up. "Look at that!
Ella's telling us that she'll keep Storm in

check. She won't let him be a pest around the farm. Way to go, old girl!"

Everyone laughed.

Beth looked at her uncle and aunt. "So, can Storm stay? He can live in my room and I'll take him home when Mom and Dad come to get me," she pleaded.

"In that case, it's fine with me. If it's okay with you, Emily," Oliver said to his wife.

Beth's aunt gave a questionable smile, but she nodded.

Beth went over and hugged her aunt and uncle. "Yay! Thanks a million!"

She felt so happy that she was even ready to forgive Martin for playing mean tricks on her, but there was still

one thing she wanted to mention to
him first.

Beth waited until she, Martin, Storm,
and Ella were walking across the fields
before bringing the subject up. "I think
you should apologize for pushing me
into Darcy's pen. It was a mean thing
to do," she exclaimed.

Martin's eyes widened. "Are you
still talking about that? Can't you take a
joke? Girls *always* make such a big deal
out of everything."

"Yes, because boys do such stupid
things!" Beth replied. "I thought Darcy
was going to charge at me. If it hadn't
been for St—Anyway, I was lucky to
get out without getting hurt."

But Martin wasn't listening. He had

turned around to wait for Ella who was lagging behind. The old collie was walking stiffly with her head drooping. "Come on, girl!" he called fondly.

At the sound of his voice, Ella tried to quicken her step, but her back legs gave way and she sat down.

"She's been doing that more and more lately," Martin said, frowning.

Beth's anger with Martin melted away as her heart filled with sadness at the sight of the sick old dog.

Storm glanced up at her with softly glowing eyes. "I will fetch Ella!" he woofed gently.

Beth stood beside Martin and they watched Storm bound down the field. As soon as Storm reached the old sheepdog, he barked encouragingly and licked Ella's gray muzzle. When she just lay there panting, Storm crouched down onto his front paws and stuck his bottom in the air, inviting her to play chase.

Martin smiled at the cute puppy's antics. "You're wasting your time, Storm. Ella's running around days are *well* over!" he called, but then his face fell and his eyes looked sad and troubled.

Beth reached out to touch his arm.

"I'm okay. Don't make a scene!" Martin said, rubbing a sleeve across his face.

Beth saw Storm running back and forth in front of Ella, woofing gently to encourage her until she finally heaved herself to her feet. As the old collie limped up the field, Storm ambled alongside her, keeping pace on his short legs.

"Here she comes. Good girl," Martin said, petting Ella's ears.

"Thanks, Storm," Beth whispered to him. "Martin might be the most annoying person in the universe, but he really loves Ella."

The four of them slowly walked back to the farmyard in silence. As they came through the gate into the yard, Martin turned to Beth. "Do you want to see the dairy?" he said more cheerfully.

Beth shrugged. "I don't care. But I thought we weren't allowed in there without permission."

"No problem. I told Mom we might go in and she was cool with it." Martin opened the door of a brick building, next to the barn. "But dogs are definitely not allowed. Stay, Ella," he ordered.

Ella sat down obediently.

"Will you wait here, please, Storm?" Beth whispered, so Martin couldn't hear. "I won't be long."

Storm immediately sat down next to Ella and lay with his nose on his paws.

Martin smiled. "Storm really catches on quickly, doesn't he? Look how he copies what Ella does. He's one bright puppy!"

Beth smiled to herself. If only Martin knew how right he was!

Inside the dairy it was cool and really clean. Beth walked around, looking at the white work surfaces, shiny metal equipment, and huge fridges, being careful not to touch anything.

But Martin was just the opposite. "I haven't been in here for so long. I forgot that some of this stuff's pretty high-tech. I wonder what these do." He began turning some dials on a big drum-shaped machine.

There was an ominous glugging noise.

"Should you be playing with that?" Beth asked worriedly.

Martin grinned. "You're such a scaredy-cat. Don't panic. I'm putting the settings back to what they were." He turned the dial again and the glugging noise got louder.

Gloop. Gloop. Whoosh! Suddenly a

fountain of milk gushed out of a
narrow chute and poured onto the
floor.

"Oh no!" Martin cried, frantically
working, but the milk only sprayed out
faster.

Beth stood there in horror as a rising
tide of milk swirled around her boots.
"Do something, Martin!"

"I'm trying to!" Martin's face was
bright red.

The door banged open and Emily Badby rushed into the dairy. Taking in the situation with one look, she marched over to the machine and adjusted the dials. Seconds later, the flow of milk slowed and then stopped.

Emily turned around with a furious look on her face.

"Beth told me to do it!" Martin cried, before his mom could speak.

Beth's jaw dropped. "No, I didn't!"

Martin smirked. "Yes, you did! Don't try and squirm your way out of it—"

"Be quiet! Both of you," Emily snapped. "I'm very disappointed in you both. You're not even supposed to be in here without permission!"

Beth glared furiously at Martin. She

was really tempted to tell her aunt how he had lied about having permission to come in here, but she'd never been a tattletale and she wasn't about to start now.

"You know the house rules perfectly well, Martin. Besides, Beth is our guest," Emily said stiffly, still furious. "What do you have to say for yourself?"

Martin shrugged. "Chill out, Mom! Don't have a major panic attack! It's only a little milk. It won't take long to clean up."

"You think so?" Emily's face darkened. "Stay there, you two! Don't you dare move!" She sloshed through the milk and opened a cabinet. "Here!" She thrust mops and buckets at Martin

and Beth. "I want that floor spotless. Do
you hear me? I'd stand and watch you,
but I have to go out now. I'll be back
in an hour, though, to check up on
you. And if you touch anything else,
Martin Badby, you'll . . . you'll be in
big trouble!"

She stormed out and a few seconds

later Beth heard a car start up and drive away.

"Oh gosh!" Beth said, letting out a huge sigh of relief. She'd never seen her aunt so angry. "I thought she was going to explode!"

"Oh, Mom's never angry for long. She'll forget all about it by this evening. You don't mind cleaning up by yourself, do you? I just remembered I've got something important to talk to Dad about," Martin said, splashing milk everywhere as he went toward the door.

"Hey! Come back—" Beth cried, but Martin had already left.

Her spirits sank as she looked down at the lake of milk. It was everywhere: under the work surfaces, sloshing around the machinery, and even leaking out under the door into the yard. She hardly knew where to begin.

"Thanks for nothing, Martin," she grumbled, angry that she'd bothered to save him from being in even more trouble with her aunt.

"I will help you, Beth!" Storm woofed eagerly from the open doorway.

Beth felt a warm prickling sensation down her spine. Something very strange was about to happen.

Chapter
FOUR

Big gold sparks ignited in Storm's fluffy black-and-white fur and his ears and tail crackled with electricity.

Storm raised a big black front paw and a spurt of golden sparks shot out and whooshed around the dairy. They zizzed around like a swarm of busy worker bees.

Beth heard a series of faint pops as a shimmering army of mops appeared out of thin air and stood at attention. As if at an invisible signal, they began mopping the floor up and down in neat

rows. In perfect time, they squeezed
their milky heads into each bucket in
turn. *Swish! Swoosh!*

"This is great!" Beth said, clapping
her hands with glee as the rows of
mops did their work.

In no time at all, the dairy floor
was spotless. The magic mops stood
at attention once more and then

disappeared in a final cascade of
golden sparks.

"Wow! Thanks, Storm, that was
awesome!" Beth went over and gave
him a cuddle.

"You are welcome," Storm barked
happily. "But I saw Martin going
into the house. Why didn't he help
you?"

"That's what I want to know," Beth
said angrily. "He made some lame
excuse about talking to his dad about
something. I've had just about enough
of my annoying cousin. Come on,
Storm, let's go and find him. I've got a
few things I want to say to him!"

Storm yapped in agreement.

As Beth charged into the house with

Storm toward the living room, she heard Uncle Ollie's voice coming through the open door and stopped in her tracks.

"It's really not fair to let Ella go on like this. She's in pain and she can barely move around. I think it's time we called the vet and put her to sleep," he was saying.

"No! Please wait, Dad. Let's leave her for just a little longer," Martin pleaded, sounding as if he was very close to tears.

"I'm sorry, Martin. I know you love Ella, but I'm not prepared to let any animal suffer, however hard it is for you to accept. We have to think what's best for Ella. Why don't we talk about it

again tomorrow. All right?" Oliver
Badby said gently.

"Okay. But I'm not changing my
mind about calling the vet and you
can't make me!" Martin said in a
choked voice.

Beth didn't wait to hear the rest of
the conversation. She already felt a little
guilty for listening. "Come on, Storm,"
she whispered, tiptoeing away.

Storm trotted at her heel as she
went into the kitchen. Beth felt her
anger drain away again, just like
when they were in the field earlier.
However annoying her cousin was,
she wouldn't wish that on anyone.

"Martin was actually telling the truth
this time. He really did want to talk to

his dad about something important. Ella must be very sick if Uncle Ollie thinks the vet should put her to sleep. Poor old girl," she said to Storm.

Storm nodded, his midnight-blue eyes sad.

Ella was curled up in her basket in the warm alcove. As Beth bent down to pet her, the old dog's tail thumped against the floor.

Beth felt tears stinging her eyes. "It's a shame that Ella's in such pain. If she wasn't, she'd be able to enjoy a few more months with Martin."

Storm pricked his ears. "I might be able to help!"

Beth blinked at him. "Really? Can you use your magic to make her young again?" she asked hopefully.

"I am sorry, Beth. No magic can do that," Storm woofed gently. He padded over and stood in front of Ella.

Once again, Beth felt the warm tingling sensation down her spine.

Big gold sparks ignited in Storm's fluffy black-and-white fur and the tips of his ears sparked with magical power. She watched as he huffed out a warm glittery breath.

A shimmering golden mist surrounded the old collie. For a few seconds, pinpricks of gold danced all around her like miniature fireflies and then they sank into Ella's dull fur and disappeared.

Beth waited expectantly, but nothing happened. Ella looked just the same, with her gray muzzle and faded eyes.

Storm's magic didn't seem to have worked.

"Never mind. You tried. I guess magic can't be expected to do everything," Beth said to Storm, trying hard to hide her disappointment as the last golden spark faded from Ella's fur. "Let's go into the living room and find Martin. He's probably feeling really upset. Maybe we can cheer him up."

Storm had a gleam in his eye, but he just nodded. "You have a very kind heart, Beth."

"Anyone would do the same," Beth said, blushing. She always got embarrassed when people gave her compliments.

Martin was lying on the sofa. Behind

it, Beth could see the cabinet displaying the cups and trophies her uncle had won in plowing competitions.

Oliver Badby sat at the table, working at the computer. He looked up and smiled as Beth and Storm came in. "Hello. What have you two been up to?"

"We . . . I've finished cleaning up all the milk in the dairy. I thought Martin might like to go out with us or something," Beth said.

Her uncle frowned and glanced at Martin. "What's that about milk?"

"Er . . . nothing!" Martin said hurriedly, getting up in a rush and pushing Beth out. "Come on, Beth. Let's go and see if Mom needs any help with her shopping."

"But she's not even back yet . . ." Beth protested, shaking off his arm.

"Duh! I know that! But Dad doesn't, does he?" Martin scoffed. "And why did you have to mention the milk?"

But once in the hall, his shoulders slumped. "Dad's been talking about taking Ella to the vet, to . . . to—"

"I know. I heard you talking to him," Beth interrupted, feeling a lump rise in her throat. "I'm so sorry."

Martin shuffled his feet. "Yeah, well. I know Ella's old and everything and I'm not ready to let her go, but Dad could be . . ." He lifted his head and looked past Beth into the kitchen. She saw an expression of complete amazement come over his face. "I don't believe it!"

"What?" Beth whipped around and saw Ella padding out of the kitchen. The old dog was moving easily. Her coat looked glossy and her eyes were bright and alert.

Ella trotted up to Martin and jumped up to be pet. "Woof!" she barked happily, wagging her tail and giving him a wide doggy grin.

"Look at her! It's like a miracle. She's

not even limping!" Martin threw his arms around Ella and hugged her, burying his face in her fur.

Ella barked, licking him all over his face.

"Just wait until Dad sees her! There's no way he'll be taking her to the vet now!" Martin's face was lit up like a Halloween pumpkin.

Beth beamed with joy as she watched the two of them. She bent down to pet Storm. "Thanks again, Storm. This time from Martin and Ella. They're going to have a great summer together," she whispered.

Storm wagged his little tail happily.

Chapter
FIVE

"Ella seems to have found a new
best friend since that puppy arrived,"
Emily Badby said as she was clearing
away lunch the following day.

Beth was helping her aunt load the
dishwasher. She smiled, wishing that
everyone knew just how true that was!
But, of course, she would never tell them
or anyone else how magical Storm was.

Oliver Badby was finishing a cup of tea
and Martin had just come back into the
kitchen after taking some food scraps
outside to the pigpen.

Storm was stretched out under the table. Suddenly his eyes flashed with mischief. Leaping out, he ran around the huge farmhouse table, his ears laid back and his tail streaming behind him.

Across the room in her bed, Ella's ears pricked up. With a spring in her step, she shot toward the silly puppy and started chasing him. Storm suddenly swerved, leaped into her empty bed, and threw himself down. Ella jumped straight in after him. Seconds later, the two of them were curled up together, licking each other.

Everyone laughed.

"That's one way to sneak into a warm bed! You know, Ella and Storm

could almost be a mother and her
puppy," Martin said fondly.

Then they heard the rumbling sound
of a heavy trucks pulling up outside in
the yard. Martin ran to the window and
looked out.

"It's here, Dad! The Fergy's arrived!"
he shouted, dashing outside.

Beth's uncle and aunt went outside to look. Beth followed curiously, wondering what was going on.

A large flatbed truck stood in the yard. On the back of it, there was a tomato-red tractor. Oliver went to speak to the truck driver and then they began the unloading. A few minutes later, the red tractor stood in the yard.

Martin walked around it, his eyes shining. "It's supercool, isn't it?"

"I guess it's okay," Beth said, shrugging. She couldn't see what was so exciting about a boring old farm machine.

"Okay?" Martin gave her an incredulous look. "Are you kidding? That's a 1952 Massey Ferguson tractor."

Beth wasn't impressed. "It's kind of old, isn't it? Does it still work?"

Her uncle chuckled. "Fergy's going to work very well. Wait until you see her pulling a plow. She's going to help me win the cup in the vintage class at the plowing competition in a few weeks."

"Dad's county champion at plowing," Martin said proudly.

To Beth, winning things for making straight lines down a field seemed like a very weird thing to do. *Don't they watch any TV around here?* she thought.

Martin saw the scornful look on her face. He blushed. "There's a lot of skill involved in plowing, you know. Dad lets me try sometimes and I'm getting really

good at it," he boasted. "I'm going to get a license when I'm fourteen. Then I can compete, too!"

"You're doing all right, but you'll need a lot more practice first," his dad said.

"I know that," Martin said in a sulky voice.

Oliver patted his son on the shoulder. "Fergy could use a wash and brush up. She's pretty dusty after her journey. Any volunteers?"

Martin's head came up. "Beth and I will do it. Won't we, Beth?"

Beth frowned. Cleaning a tractor was definitely not on the top of her "fun to do" list. It was right at the bottom, next to cleaning smelly sneakers. But Martin seemed in an unusually good mood, so she nodded.

"Okay. I don't mind." *But if he starts bossing me around again, I'm leaving him to do it*, she thought.

Beth helped Martin collect buckets, sponges, and cleaning liquid. Storm came outside and lay down with his chin resting on his paws as she and Martin started work.

"There's all kinds of plowing, you know. Tractor-trailed, mounted, reversible. You have to be very skilled to work a plot and make perfect ins and outs," Martin explained enthusiastically as he sponged soapy water over Fergy's bright-red hood. "They have world championship competitions. One day Dad might be good enough to participate."

Beth didn't reply. She was scrubbing hard at a greasy mark on Fergy's red grill.

"Hey! Are you listening? Or are you ignoring me on purpose?" Martin flicked soapy water at her.

"Who said that?" Beth joked and
flicked water back at him.

Martin's eyes gleamed mischievously.
"Oh yeah!"

Beth dodged out of the way as
another sponge full of water flew
toward her. "Missed!" she teased.

Laughing, they flicked soapy water back and forth.

Beth giggled as she pushed her damp hair out of her eyes and crouched behind the tractor. She was smaller than Martin and managed to avoid getting too wet, but most of her soapy flicks found their mark.

Martin's T-shirt was soon drenched. "Right! Now you're in for it!" He grabbed the whole bucket and lifted it into the air.

"Don't you dare!" Beth shrieked breathlessly.

As she went to flick more water at Martin, a tiny shower of golden sparks crackled around her hand and tingled against her fingers. The soapy sponge

shot out of her hand. It zoomed
through the air with perfect aim and
splatted in Martin's face.

"Phoof!" Martin spluttered. He took a
step backward and slipped over onto his
backside, tipping the entire bucket of
water all over himself.

Beth cracked up laughing. She was
helpless. She glanced across at Storm
who wore a wide doggy grin and
wagged her finger at him, scolding him
gently.

"Sorry, Beth. I thought he was going
to hurt you!" Storm yapped.

Scowling, Martin slowly got up. His
dark hair was plastered to his head and
water was dripping off the end of his
nose.

Beth tried to stop laughing at the
look on Martin's face, but her mouth
kept twitching. "You should see
yourself," she gasped, holding her ribs.

Suddenly Martin burst out laughing,
too. "That was a great shot—for a girl!
Come on, let's get some clean water."

Beth went with him to fill her bucket
from the outside tap. Staying at Tail End

Farm was starting to feel a lot better these days.

She was amazed at Martin. This was the most friendly he'd been since she arrived. And all because they'd had a water fight and she'd beaten him. *I'll never understand boys*, she thought as they finished cleaning the tractor.

Chapter
SIX

Beth stood in the barn beside her
aunt and watched her milking the goats.
Storm was sprawled on a pile of clean
straw beside the pens.

Beth sighed. It had rained almost
every day since she'd been here. Heavy
rain was drumming on the roof once
again. "I'm getting fed up with this
terrible weather," she complained.

Emily smiled. "You learn to deal with
it when you work on a farm. But the
goats really hate the cold and the wet.
That's why I brought them into the

barn, but I'd hoped they could go out
in their field again by now." She looked
at her niece's sad face. "Do you want to
try milking?"

"I don't know," Beth said doubtfully.

"Come on. Don't be shy. Stand here.
It's not very difficult and Daisy's a good
milker," Emily encouraged. She showed
Beth how to take a firm but gentle
hold and squeeze down with one finger
at a time.

Beth took a deep breath and rested one shoulder against Daisy's flank. She followed instructions, a bit awkwardly at first. To her surprise, the milk began to flow into the bucket.

"Hey! I'm doing it!" she cried delightedly.

In a few minutes Beth felt like an expert. She filled a bucket and then strained the milk into the metal churn, feeling really pleased with her success. "That was great. Maybe I'll ask Mom and Dad if we can have some goats. It would save Dad moaning about having to dig up all the weeds and we'd have tons of milk to give to all our friends."

"Hmm. Remember that you'd have to milk them twice a day, summer and winter, seven days a week, in all kinds of weather, just like I do," her aunt cautioned, smiling.

Beth raised her eyebrows. "On second thought, I think I'll stick to milk in cartons and leave the weeds to Dad!"

Her aunt laughed.

A loud triumphant braying came from the back of the barn. There was a stamping and clattering, followed by a rustling noise.

"Darcy?! What's he doing?" Beth asked.

"It sounds like he's jumped out of his pen—again," her aunt sighed. "That goat's a real menace. He's been cooped up for too long because of all this rain and he's got energy to spare. It's going to be really hard to catch him."

"Can I help you?" Beth offered.

"You could go and see where Darcy's gone, if you like, while I close the barn door so he can't escape," her aunt said.

"I will find Darcy!" Storm barked, darting to the back of the barn.

Beth hurried after him. As she reached the big stack of straw bales near the goat's pen, she spotted Darcy standing right on the very top of them.

"Look at him! He thinks he's the king of the castle!" Beth said.

Looking down his haughty nose, Darcy snickered as if he agreed. He looked very pleased with himself for having climbed up so high.

Storm wagged his tail and then

jumped up onto his back legs and put his front paws on the bottom bale. "Gr-oof!" his bright eyes flashed playfully.

"Watch out, Storm. That stack looks a little wobbly—" Beth began, but before she could finish her sentence, Darcy flexed his powerful back legs and did an almighty leap in the air, right over Beth and Storm's heads—and then everything seemed to happen all at once.

The top straw bale shook wildly from the force of Darcy's takeoff and slowly began to tip forward.

Beth's eyes widened in horror. Storm had turned his head to watch Darcy land on the barn floor a few feet away and hadn't noticed the danger. The bale was about to fall and land on him!

Without a second thought, Beth
threw herself forward. Her fingers just
touched Storm's fluffy black-and-white
fur and she managed to grab him.
Holding him close to her chest Beth
rolled out of the way just in time. The

heavy bale crashed to the ground and she felt the rush of dusty air as it missed them both by a fraction of an inch.

Beth let out a shaky sigh of relief. Still holding Storm, she pushed herself slowly to her feet. "Are you all right?" she asked the shocked little puppy.

"Yes. You saved me, Beth. Thank you," Storm woofed, reaching up to lick her chin.

"I couldn't bear anything happening to you," Beth said as she pet Storm's soft ears. She felt a surge of affection for her tiny friend.

Glancing down the barn, Beth saw that her aunt had managed to get a rope on a subdued-looking Darcy and was leading him back to his pen. She frowned when she reached Beth and Storm and saw the straw bale on the floor nearby. "I thought I heard something fall, but I couldn't be sure with all the noise Darcy was making. Are you okay? You're lucky you weren't badly hurt," she said.

"Oh, it missed us by miles," Beth said lightly, not wanting to worry her aunt.

"Thank goodness for that!" Emily

said, relieved. "I'm responsible for you while you're here and your mom and dad wouldn't be very happy with me if you had an accident. I'll get Oliver to come and fix that stack. Just let me tether this naughty goat in his pen first. He's full of surprises."

Beth bit back a grin. *He's not the only one!* she thought.

"I'm sorry, Martin, I don't have time to go out with you today. Maybe tomorrow. I'm planning to clear the unused part of the top field and use that for practicing plowing, but I can't promise when I'll get around to it," Oliver was saying.

"Aw, Da-ad. You've already been out

on Fergy a couple of times. When am I going to get the chance to take a drive?"

Beth sat in the window seat in the living room with Storm curled on a cushion beside her. Her uncle and cousin were in the yard outside. Their voices floated in through the open window. "Martin's obsessed with that dumb old red tractor, even though Uncle Ollie told him it's too big for him to drive by himself."

Storm's ears twitched and he gave a sleepy nod, tired out from all the excitement in the barn earlier.

Two minutes later, Martin burst into the room and threw himself down next to Beth.

"Watch it! You almost sat on Storm!" Beth complained.

"Sorry, Storm." Martin pet Storm's fluffy black-and-white fur absently. "Dad's being a big pain! He won't let me near Fergy unless he's with me. I know I can handle driving her by myself, but he won't believe me," he grumbled.

Beth wisely chose to stay silent on the subject. "It finally stopped raining. Why don't we walk into the village with Storm and Ella?" she suggested, trying to cheer him up.

Martin's lip curled. "Go shopping? I'd rather watch paint dry. I'm going to take Ella for a long walk over the fields. By myself," he said rudely.

Beth got the message. She didn't
bother to tell him that she was about to
suggest that they go to the new sports
center. "Suit yourself." She shrugged,
got up, and called to Storm to follow
her.

"Where are you going?" Martin
asked, frowning.

Beth turned to him and tapped the
side of her nose with one finger in
what she knew was an annoying way.

Martin threw up his hands, got up, and stormed out, muttering about "stupid annoying girls" under his breath.

"Oh well. Martin's back to his usual self. His good mood didn't last long, did it?" Beth said to Storm. "But I'm getting used to him now and I don't mind it so much. I think he just likes complaining!"

Storm nodded, blinking up at her with bright midnight-blue eyes.

Beth changed her mind about the sports center. "We'll go to the village by ourselves. I bet they have a pet shop that sells dog treats," she decided.

Storm yelped excitedly, almost falling over his own paws as he bounded out of the door.

Chapter
SEVEN

Emily Badby had been baking bread all morning and the whole farmhouse smelled wonderful.

Beth sat in the cozy kitchen, reading a new computer magazine she'd bought at the village shop. Storm was curled up under the table, chewing on a bone-shaped dog chew, and Beth could feel the tiny puppy's warmth against her feet.

It had just been raining again, but a watery sun was now beginning to push through the clouds.

Suddenly the faint sound of barking

and growling interrupted Beth's
peaceful morning. She tensed up,
listening hard. It seemed to be coming
from far away, but then the noise
stopped and Beth thought she must
have been mistaken. Her aunt didn't
seem to have noticed anything.

"Where's Martin?" Beth asked.

"Up at the top field. His dad's starting
to clear it with Fergy and the old plow.
Ella's with him," Emily replied.

Making sure her aunt wasn't looking,
Beth leaned over to whisper to Storm.
"I'll take you for a walk up there later.
It's no good waiting for Martin and
Ella to come back here. Wild horses
wouldn't drag him away if Uncle Ollie's
plowing."

There was no reply.

Frowning, Beth bent over and looked
under the table. Storm was gone,
leaving the half-eaten dog chew lying
there.

That was odd. He'd never run off
without telling her where he was going

before. She got up and went to look for
him.

Storm wasn't in the living room or
any of the other downstairs rooms. She
went up to her bedroom, expecting to
find him curled up on her blanket, but
he wasn't there either.

"Storm?" she said, beginning to feel
concerned.

A faint sound came from under her
pillows. Beth smiled and pulled back
the top of the blanket to reveal a little
black-and-white tail. "What's this, hide-
and-seek—" she began, but stopped at
the sight of Storm trembling all over.
"What's wrong? Are you sick?" she
asked worriedly.

Storm squirmed farther into the

pillows. "I sense that Shadow knows where I am. He will send his magic, so that any dogs that are nearby will attack me," he said in a muffled little whine.

"Oh no! That must have been what I heard. We need to find you a better hiding place. Maybe the barn or . . . or . . ." Beth tried to think of somewhere safe.

"It is no use, Beth," Storm whimpered, his deep-blue eyes as dull as stones. "Leave me here for a while, please. Any dogs looking for me may pass by."

"All right. If that's what you want," Beth said. She had a sudden thought. "What about Ella? Will Shadow's magic work on her, too?" She felt horrified

that the gentle old collie might become
Storm's enemy.

"No. I have already used my magic to
help her. That will protect Ella from
Shadow's evil ways," Storm whined
before he burrowed right under the
pillows and curled up into a tight little
ball.

Beth gently gathered his tail in,
replaced the blanket, and tucked it
tightly around him. No one would

know there was anything under the pillow. She went out quietly, hoping that Storm's plan would work. She couldn't bear to think of her friend having to leave suddenly without warning.

Beth could hardly eat any lunch because she was so worried about Storm. She nibbled on a few mouthfuls of salad and cauliflower and then asked if she could leave the table.

"Are you feeling all right?" her aunt asked.

"Fine, thanks. I'm just not very hungry," Beth replied.

Martin glanced at Beth in concern and seemed about to say something, but then he changed his mind. He finished eating and jumped up from the table.

"Why don't you and Storm come up to the top field before lunch and see how Dad and I are doing? We've cleared a lot of it already. I'm going up there again now with Ella. You could come with us, if you like."

"I might. I'll . . . um . . . follow you up there in a minute," Beth murmured absently.

"Whatever," Martin muttered.

When he and Ella had left, Beth went into the hall with a heavy heart. She was dreading going upstairs to her bedroom. Would Storm still be here or had her friend already left forever?

Suddenly, a tiny fluffy black-and-white figure came bounding down the stairs.

"Hello, Beth," Storm barked happily.

"Storm! You're still here!" Beth cried, overjoyed, throwing her arms around him.

Storm yapped and licked her face, his tail moving wildly. His midnight-blue eyes were as bright as a moonlit sky and he seemed completely back to his usual self. "I cannot sense any strange dogs nearby, so they must have gone away. But if they return I might have to leave at once. We might not have time to say good-bye."

"I understand," Beth said, hardly taking this in. She just wanted to enjoy every single moment of the time they could spend together now.

She secretly hoped that Storm would stay with her forever, even though she knew he must someday return to help his

injured mother and lead the Moon-
claw wolf pack.

Beth decided to talk about something
else. "Do you want to go watch Uncle
Ollie giving Martin some plowing
practice? It'll probably be really boring,"
she said, making a face.

Storm's cute face lit up, as it always
did at any chance of a walk.

Where's Uncle Ollie? Beth wondered as
they walked toward the top field. She
could see the red tractor and the plow
mounted behind it, but only Martin
and Ella stood beside it.

Storm was trotting beside her with
his nose sniffing around on the ground.

Martin waved. "Hi! I didn't think

you'd come," he shouted, sounding
surprised and pleased.

Ella spotted Storm. She wagged her
tail and trotted over, barking a greeting.

"I thought we might as well. Storm
loves playing with Ella," Beth said,
smiling at the dogs.

"Great. Now you can see what
plowing's all about. Watch this," Martin
called out. Leaping into Fergy's seat he
started the engine and moved forward.

"Martin, don't! You're not supposed to

be doing that!" Beth said worriedly, remembering her uncle's strict rules about Martin only driving under his supervision.

"I know what I'm doing!" Martin said huffily. "Anyway, I'll only plow a couple of furrows. Dad just went down to the barn for a can of lubricating oil—he'll never know. Unless you decide to tell him," he said, looking harshly at her.

"Thanks a lot. You should know by now that I don't tell!" Beth said indignantly.

Martin looked uncomfortable and then he gave a grin and nodded. Concentrating hard, he held the large steering wheel steady as the red tractor trundled slowly along, pulling the plow behind it. As he moved forward, the weedy ground was turned over and the soil curved away from the plow's metal moldboards in rich brown waves.

Despite herself, Beth was fascinated by watching the furrows form. Martin leaned over to watch the back wheels, making sure he kept driving in a perfectly straight line. The new brown furrow folded itself over and was laid neatly next to one previously made.

Beth realized that plowing took a lot of skill. "You're pretty good at this, aren't you?" she said, impressed.

Martin threw her a smile over his shoulder, obviously enjoying himself and pleased by her praise. "I'm not bad. But then I was taught by an expert. My dad!"

Suddenly Storm's head came up and

his midnight-blue eyes flashed. Barking shrilly, he raced forward and began darting back and forth in front of Fergy's front wheels. "Stop! Stop!" he barked urgently.

"Martin! Watch out for Storm!" Beth cried.

"Why's he doing that? Make him stop!" Martin shouted.

Beth frowned. It wasn't like Storm to do something so dangerous without a good reason. But she was too worried about him getting hurt to try and figure out what that was.

"Come here, Storm! You'll get hurt!" she shouted.

But Storm seemed determined. Barking frantically, he ran even closer to the tractor's ridged tires, snapping at them and growling. One of the wheels passed by him closely, missing him by a fraction.

As a stone flew out and hit him, Storm gave a loud yelp.

"Martin! Look out!" Beth screamed, thinking that Storm was about to be run over.

Panicking, Martin jerked the tractor's steering wheel to avoid the tiny puppy. Fergy rolled to a halt. Martin turned off the engine and jumped down.

"Look at that furrow. It's all messed up now. That stupid puppy made me mess up!" he fumed.

Storm stood by, panting heavily, his little sides heaving.

"Hang on! What's that? Look!" Beth interrupted, pointing at something half buried in a weedy grass ditch that Martin had been just about to plow over. As Beth leaned over for a closer look, her heart missed a beat. "I think it might be a firecracker!"

Chapter
EIGHT

"Don't be crazy!" Martin said to Beth, walking over to take a look, but the moment he saw the metal object he frowned. "Oh! You're right. It does look like a firecracker. But it's probably been there for a while. Look, it's all shriveled and dented. I bet it's harmless."

"Storm didn't seem to think so," Beth reminded him.

Martin hesitated, chewing at his lip.

Beth guessed that he was worried about getting into trouble for driving the tractor. "Martin, this is an

emergency. We have to go and tell
Uncle Ollie—now!" she said.

"You're right," Martin decided.
"Come on!"

Beth didn't need to be told twice.
She bent down to pick up Storm and
then turned on her heel and ran.
Martin and Ella leaped after her and

they all hurried back toward the farm
as fast as they could.

Luckily Oliver was just coming
out of the barn with an oil can. He
raised his eyebrows when they raced
straight up to him. "Where's the fire?"
he joked, but his face grew serious as
Martin and Beth began explaining.

"Good job, you two. You did the
right thing. Firecrackers need expert
handling. I'll call the emergency services
and then alert the neighbors." He took
his cell phone out of his jacket pocket
and dialed. "Martin, will you go into
the house and tell your mom, please?"

Martin nodded, his face now pale
with worry.

Beth realized that her cousin had only

just begun to grasp how serious this really was. Now that they were all a safe distance from the firecracker, she found herself shaking as it all sank in.

"Thank goodness you sensed the firecracker was there. You were very brave to get so close to the tractor and risk getting hurt," she whispered to Storm.

"I had to stop Martin somehow. We were too close for me to use my magic. Martin would have seen, but I could not risk anyone getting hurt," Storm woofed gently.

Beth and Storm stood in the yard with Martin, Ella, and her aunt as noisy police cars and fire engines arrived. Farm workers and their families began gathering, too.

Beth looked toward the top field, where the lights from half a dozen police cars were now flashing. She could see at least four fire engines. Bright-yellow hazard tape had been put up all around the site of the firecracker and across the field entrance.

"If it hadn't been for Storm, I'd have plowed right over that firecracker," Martin said. He bent down to pat Storm's head. "Thanks, boy. You might have just saved my life."

"You are welcome, Martin," Storm barked, wagging his tail, but of course only Beth could hear him speaking.

She beamed down at Storm, feeling very proud of her brave little friend.

Oliver came up and put a hand on

his son's shoulder. "I should ground you for a week for driving Fergy when I specifically told you not to!" he said sternly.

"It wasn't my fault. Beth . . ." Martin started to make another excuse to get himself out of trouble, but then he seemed to think otherwise and hung his head. "Beth told me I shouldn't be driving Fergy by myself and she was right. I'm sorry, Dad."

"You always are," Oliver sighed. "But on this occasion it was lucky for all of us that things turned out this way. If I'd have been plowing and not you, I probably wouldn't have seen the firecracker until it was too late."

Martin looked subdued as he took

this in and realized what it could have meant. He was silent for a moment, and then he brightened. "So I'm not in all that much trouble after all. Cool!"

"I give up!" His dad shook his head slowly and rolled his eyes.

"Look, someone in the field's waving a red flag," Beth noticed.

Just then Oliver's cell phone rang. He

answered it and then spoke in a loud voice. "Listen up, everyone. There's going to be a controlled explosion in a few minutes. We shouldn't be alarmed. We're safe here."

Whump! A loud bang split the air.

Despite the early warning, Beth almost jumped out of her skin as the explosion echoed in her ears. An enormous spray of dark soil shot out in all directions and a thick dark smoke drifted upward.

"Yay! Way to go!" Martin shouted.

Everyone clapped and cheered. The danger was over.

"There'll be no more plowing in that field until the firemen have declared it safe. Do you hear me, Martin?" Oliver said.

"I wouldn't go up there now if you paid me," Martin said.

Beth could see that he meant it this time. Martin really seemed to be changing and Beth realized that she'd actually grown to like her grumpy cousin during her time at Tail End Farm!

"If you'd all like to come into the house I'll make coffee and there's freshly made cake," Emily called out to everyone.

People began filing into the farmhouse. Martin called Ella and they followed them in. Beth was about to go in, too, when Storm suddenly barked with terror and ran toward the barn.

Beth heard a fierce growl behind her

and looked around. She spotted two
scary dogs running into the farmyard.
As Beth saw their extra-long teeth and
pale wolf-like eyes, she felt very fearful.

The dogs were under Shadow's spell.
Storm's enemy had found him!

Without a second thought, Beth raced

into the barn ahead of the dogs. Somehow she knew where Storm would be. Darcy's pen!

She reached the pen at the back of the barn in time to see the tiny black-and-white puppy running into it. As the dogs pursuing Storm ran into the barn, there was a snort of rage and Darcy leaped right over the top bar of the pen and landed on the barn floor.

Braying threateningly, the billy goat ran straight at the fierce dogs with his head lowered. *Bang! Thud!* He butted them in the side, buying Storm precious time.

Suddenly there was a blinding gold flash and bright golden sparks rained down all around Beth and crackled onto the barn floor. Storm was no longer a tiny black-

and-white puppy but instead stood before her as a young silver-gray wolf with glowing midnight-blue eyes. At his side was a huge she-wolf with a gentle face.

Beth knew the moment had come when Storm had to leave.

Storm lifted his magnificent head and looked at her with sad eyes. "Be of good heart, Beth. You have been a true friend," he growled in a deep velvety voice. He raised a large silver paw in farewell and then he and his mother faded and were gone.

There was a terrifying howl of rage behind Beth. The dogs' teeth and eyes instantly returned to normal and they ran out of the barn.

Beth stood alone in the barn. A deep sadness welled up in her. She couldn't believe that Storm had left so suddenly. She was glad he was safe, but she was going to miss him terribly.

"I'll never forget you, Storm," she whispered, her throat closing with tears.

She knew that she'd always treasure the time she had shared with the tiny magic puppy.

She heard steps behind her and turned to see Darcy coming toward her. He leaned forward to nuzzle her arm. "You were really brave. Storm would be so proud of you," she said, petting him before leading him back to his pen. "The sun's coming out. I think I'll ask Aunt Em if you can go out in the field."

Darcy snickered delightedly as if he understood.

"Talking to yourself again?" Martin joked from behind her. "Are you coming into the farmhouse? I saved you a piece of cake."

As Beth turned to look at her cousin, she grinned. *Trust Martin to have the last word*, she thought, knowing somehow that Storm was watching them, his midnight-blue eyes glowing with approval.

About the Author

Sue Bentley's books for children often include animals, fairies, and wildlife. She lives in Northampton and enjoys reading, going to the movies, relaxing by her garden pond, and watching the birds feeding their babies on the lawn. At school she was always getting yelled at for daydreaming or staring out of the window— but she now realizes that she was storing up ideas for when she became a writer. She has met and owned many cats and dogs, and each one has brought a special kind of magic to her life.

Magic Puppy

Read all of the other books
in the Magic Puppy series!